ANGRY BIRDS™

Stella

WILLOW TAKES THE STAGE

EGMONT
We bring stories to life

First published in Great Britain 2015
by Egmont UK Limited
The Yellow Building, 1 Nicholas Road, London W11 4AN

Written by Elina Rouhiainen
Translated by Ruth Urbom
Illustrated by Diana Egea
Graphic designer: Terhi Haikonen

ISBN 978 1 4052 7883 6
61437/2
Printed in Malaysia

Translation rights arranged by Elina Ahlback Literary Agency.

ANGRY BIRDS™

Stella

WILLOW TAKES THE STAGE

←STELLA is the leader of the flock. She likes things done her way, but is always on the lookout for fun!

DAHLIA is the brains of the group! Is there anything she doesn't know? The quickest way to upset her is by disturbing her experiments. →

←WILLOW loves nature and is a true artist. She dreams big but is shy, and she often keeps her ideas inside her big striped hat.

POPPY is wild, funny and she loves practical jokes! The life and soul of the gang or a total goofball, depending on your mood ...

LUCA is the baby of the bunch. He thinks he's a bigger boy than he actually is, which sometimes lands him in trouble.

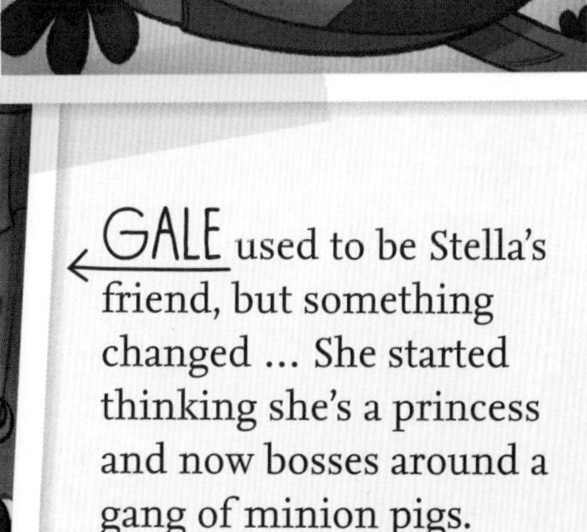

GALE used to be Stella's friend, but something changed ... She started thinking she's a princess and now bosses around a gang of minion pigs.

This diary belongs to:

Date: MONDAY

Today's the day I start keeping a diary. I've thought about doing it for a long time, but it wasn't until today that something happened to make me think I ought to write it down. I'm still kind of in shock. In fact, I'm still shaking, but maybe I'll calm down once I get it all down on paper.

First though, I should probably introduce myself. My name's Willow. I love art and the outdoors. And hats! I'm wearing my favourite hat right now. It has orange and yellow stripes. It's big and warm and almost totally covers my head feathers. I love it!!!

I ♡ MY HAT!!!

I have four fantastic friends: Stella, Poppy, Dahlia and Luca. If I had to appoint one of us as leader of our group, it would be Stella. She's brave and pretty. Poppy's good at making noise. Any noise at all … Dahlia's smart. Maybe a little too smart! Sometimes the rest of us have to remind her we don't understand half the stuff she says. Usually she says we don't need to understand; it's just that thinking out loud helps her own thought processes. All we have to do is nod. And then there's Luca. He's only little, but he's still fun to have around. He's as cute as a button!

I'm the quiet one in our group. Well ... Luca can't talk yet, but he still manages to make a lot of noise. It's not that I'm shy, I'd just rather listen than talk myself.

I'm pretty sensitive. I hate arguments and anything that might hurt people's feelings. Sometimes it feels like the others have a hard time understanding me, but fortunately those moments don't last very long.

We all live on Golden Island, which is an amazing place. We've got everything we need: trees, beaches, swimming holes and waterfalls. You could say it was a paradise. But! There are also pigs living here. The pigs ruin everything that gets in their way.

They cut down trees and rip up shrubs. There's nothing they leave untouched. I just don't get it! Why do those pigs have to behave like that? Don't they care about our world?

Date: TUESDAY

Dear Diary,

~~Are you sure you don't mind if I call you 'Diary'? I haven't bothered to come up with a better name for you. I mean, I know you're not a real person – I'm just talking to myself here, but somehow it still feels a little weird. It's a lot easier if I imagine I'm writing a letter. Once I even tried sending a letter in a bottle, but I never got an answer.~~

Yesterday I got up and went to the beach before sunrise. I wanted to paint the view from the beach – did I already tell you I love to paint? Anyway, I sat down and waited for the sun to appear from below the horizon so I could capture its hues as accurately as possible. I had just unpacked my paints and brushes when the sun's rays started to peek out from behind the ocean. It was so beautiful that, for a moment, the only thing I could do was gaze at it. Then I remembered why I was there and started mixing some paint colours. I had just done the outlines of the beach and the waves when I noticed a dark shape that stood out against the sand.

I didn't know what it was. Anyway, I didn't have any time to waste. The sun was still rising, so I tried to focus on painting its colours.

However, the dark shape just beyond the breaking waves kept distracting me. My imagination was running wild and I couldn't concentrate on my painting at all. Eventually, I had to stop working on it.

I went over to investigate. The bundle was black and covered in gunk. For a second, I was afraid it might be alive, but when it didn't move, I decided to be brave and bent down for a closer look.

I poked the bundle and then backed off, ready to flee, but when it still didn't move, I went over to check it out.

Litter. It was nothing but rubbish.

It was ugly. That litter was ruining the whole landscape, and it made me feel sad all of a sudden. I wanted it to go away. So annoying!

I didn't know what to do. The beach was totally deserted. There was nobody around who could help me in that tough situation.

Trembling, I took hold of it. It felt a little like fabric or paper, but shinier and slimier.

I wanted to get rid of it as soon as I could, but I didn't have a clue what I should do with it. So I rushed home with the litter and hid it under my bed. I couldn't see it anymore, but it was still haunting my thoughts. I knew it was there, and when I went to sleep that night, I had a nightmare. ☹

Date: WEDNESDAY

Dear Diary,

Yesterday I told you about the litter that had washed up on the beach. Well, now I have more to tell. This morning, I went back to the beach to work on my painting some more. To my surprise, more litter had appeared on the beach. And there was a LOT more than last time!

I went back to my treehouse. We all live in the same tree, and there are slides and ramps leading from every branch into a shared space in the middle.

'Wake up, everybody!' I yelled.

Then I had to wait. There was no sign of movement in the branches. Then the leaves started to rustle.

Stella was the first to zoom into the common area. Looking at her, you'd never guess she'd just woken up. Dahlia was the next to arrive.

She looked a little preoccupied, but that didn't necessarily mean anything. Dahlia is always thinking about something. Poppy was the last one to show up, and she gave a huge yawn. She had even brought her drumsticks along and started playing air drums. Then her eyelids flickered shut and I could hear her snoring. Couldn't she just concentrate a little? I thought.

'What is it?' Stella asked.

'Follow me,' I said. 'Poppy, wake up!'

I led them down to the beach. We stopped a few feet away from all the litter that had washed up on the beach overnight. The sun was already high enough that we could see some multicoloured goo dripping onto the sand. It was a disgusting sight. My eyes welled up with tears.

'Yesterday I found some litter on the beach. I took it away, but after last night there's even more!'

'What is it?' Poppy asked, in a serious voice for once.

Dahlia frowned and inspected the stuff. 'It looks like material made from some kind of synthetic or semi-synthetic polymer.'

'And what on earth does that mean?' Stella asked.

'It's plastic,' Dahlia replied.

'How did all this litter end up here?' I wondered out loud.

'Isn't it as plain as the beak on your face? It washed up out of the ocean.'

'I know that. But why? How did it get into the ocean?'

'Somebody wanted to get rid of it,' Poppy said. 'I wouldn't want that rubbish in my house, either!'

Somebody wanted to get rid of it, just like we did now. By throwing the litter into the ocean, that somebody made their problem into our problem. How selfish! What if the plastic got eaten by a whale? What if something else bad happened, besides me having nightmares – which is bad enough in itself. I hate nightmares!

'What should we do?' I didn't even try to hide the worry in my voice. 'If more and more plastic keeps turning up, soon our beach will be ruined.'

'We could throw it back into the ocean,' Poppy said.

Stella wasn't convinced. 'So it would just wash up here again? I don't think so.'

'We could bury it,' Poppy suggested.

'Plastic doesn't break down naturally, but you might be able to burn it,' Dahlia chirped.

‘Do you guys remember the last time we tried to burn something?’ Poppy asked.

Well, I remembered. Dahlia wanted to see how flammable the lighter fluid she’d developed was. The results of the test: really flammable! The shrubs caught fire, and it was pure luck that we managed to put out the flames before they reached our tree.

In the worst-case scenario, the fire could have spread to the trees and burned everything

around the whole island. The very thought made me hide under my hat.

'No, we're not going to burn anything,' I said from underneath my hat.

'I could put it to practical use,' Dahlia said.

'Like what?' Stella asked.

'Anything,' Dahlia replied.

Anything. That's such a huge category, Diary. What could Dahlia do with a pile of random rubbish? To tell you the truth, she didn't seem to be anywhere near as scared of it as me. In fact, I think she was actually excited, which made me feel a little embarrassed. I have a hard time seeing litter as anything but gross. But maybe it doesn't have to be that way!

Date: THURSDAY

Hey, Diary!

Right now, I have seven hats. There are a lot of great things about hats. I'll list all the pluses and minuses I can think of:

PLUSES

+ They keep you warm.
+ You never have to think about how to do your feathers.
+ They're always stylish!
+ A hat is a hiding place you can take with you.
+ It's like getting your brain hugged all the time.

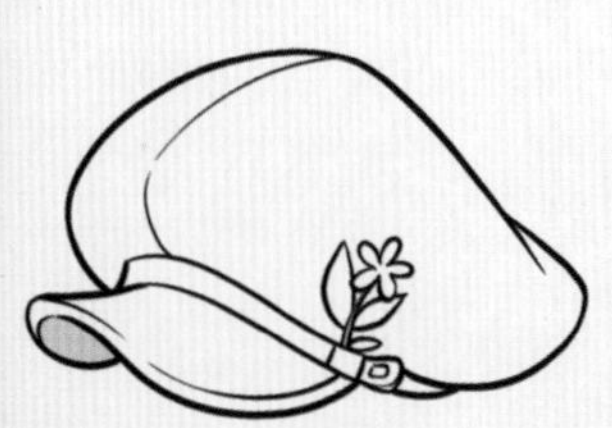

MINUSES

— Prejudice: some say it's bad manners to wear hats indoors. They're wrong!!!

LATER

There were noises coming from Dahlia's branch today. There's nothing strange about that, because she always has some project on the go. She builds all kinds of weird gadgets and does chemical experiments that usually result in either a great new invention or a cloud of smoke, which means she has to sleep over at Stella's place for a couple of nights. As you can understand, we stay far away from her branch when she's at work.

This time, though, I knew her experiment must have something to do with the litter on the beach. My curiosity got the better of me. I reached under my bed and took out the rubbish I'd hidden there the other day. Now, in the full light of day, I felt a little embarrassed that I'd been so scared of it. The scraps of plastic were clearly – well, just scraps of plastic. I picked up the bundle and went over to Dahlia's treehouse.

I realised I wasn't the only one who was curious. When I went inside, I saw Stella was already there. Luca chirped a cheerful hello, and I rushed over to give him a hug.

'How's it going?' I asked.

I looked around. The room was full of rubbish. Dahlia had spread it out everywhere. Bearing in mind the amount of stuff Dahlia normally has in there, it was really crowded.

Dahlia herself was sitting at the table, examining one piece of plastic under the microscope. She was so absorbed in her work, she didn't even notice me come in.

'OK, I think,' Stella replied. 'Dahlia still hasn't said a word.'

Poppy appeared in the doorway. If Dahlia's place was crowded before, it was really jam-packed now. We watched Dahlia putter around for a while until our patience finally ran out.

'Dahlia,' Stella ventured.

No reaction.

Poppy hopped up in front of Dahlia. 'Dahlia. DAHLIA!'

Dahlia looked up. She blinked. 'Oh, you're all here.'

Stella, Poppy, and I exchanged glances. Stella said, 'Yes, we are. We want to know how the project's going. Have you figured out what you want to do with the litter yet?'

'Not yet. First I numbered every single piece we found on the beach and examined their contents and characteristics. Then I made a chart of my findings.'

I looked at the chaos surrounding us. Dahlia has an amazing ability to organise things on paper and in her head, but not in her home.

'There's an awful lot of rubbish,' Stella remarked.

'Maybe we should use it to make something for all of us,' I suggested.

'Like what?' Poppy asked.

I looked around. I couldn't help noticing the expectant atmosphere in Dahlia's treehouse. There was something humming under the surface. I soon realised what it was: excitement.

Recently, our lives had been pretty calm (well, as calm as things can be for four adventurous girls!). It was only now that I realised we'd been longing for a new adventure. Now something had happened, and we didn't yet know what it would lead to.

So exciting!!

'Well, as materials, these pieces are kind of similar to fabric,' Dahlia began.

'CLOTHES!' Poppy exclaimed. 'Let's make clothes out of them!'

'Yeah!'

'Brilliant idea!'

It really was a brilliant idea. I mean, who doesn't like clothes? ~~Or new hats – even though there's no way new hats could ever replace someone's favourite hat~~. Maybe we could put on a fashion show. ~~Maybe there could be hats in it, too~~. I'm not exactly sure what we'll do yet, but this seems so great! Now we can take some time to dream and plan. There's still time before everything gets underway.

Date: FRIDAY

Dear Diary,

I have a news flash about our clothing project. Guess what? We're gonna put on a fashion show! I'm so excited!!! ☺

A LITTLE LATER

Well … Now I've calmed down enough to be able to tell you what happened earlier. You see, I have written a play. Actually, I've written quite a few plays, but this is about my Big Play. I wrote it a while ago but didn't tell anybody about it.

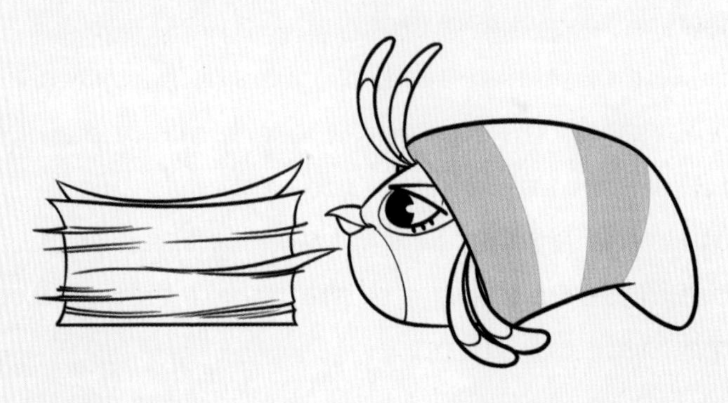

I wasn't brave enough. There's nobody on this island who'd be interested. At least that's what I thought. Turns out I was totally mistaken.

Yesterday we were going through the rubbish that had washed up on the beach. Dahlia had already investigated all of it really carefully, and she assured us we could make absolutely anything out of it.

So we started making plans. Stella and Poppy were brainstorming out loud.

'I'd like to have a tulle skirt,' Stella said.

'We don't have any tulle. But don't you think this sack would make a nice leather jacket?' Poppy asked excitedly.

'You'd get hot in it,' Dahlia chirped.

'Pah!' Poppy snorted.

I kept quiet and worked on my drawing. I let my ideas take flight and drew all kinds of dresses.

At one point, Stella peeked over my shoulder. 'Those don't look like everyday clothes. Are you designing outfits for a costume party?' she asked.

Poppy burst out laughing. She held up a big piece of ragged green plastic. 'You could make this into a pig suit.'

Pig suit. Those were the key words that unlocked my imagination. My heart started racing. There was ~~one dream~~ a little idea I'd had for a long time. OK, I have a lot of ideas, but at that moment one of them stood out above the others. And then I heard myself saying it out loud: 'I've written a play that has pigs in it.'

'A play?' Dahlia asked. She looked a little confused.

I nodded. 'Yeah. There are five characters in it. It's about a princess who saves her realm from some pigs.' I looked at my friends. I couldn't tell what they were thinking from their expressions. Maybe they weren't thinking anything. Help!

An opportunity was staring me right in the face, and I knew it might vanish any second. I just had to tell them about it, even though I needed to take a deep breath before I could speak. 'I just wrote it for fun. I wasn't planning to perform it, but it just occurred to me now when you guys were talking about pigs and costumes.' I realised I was babbling, so I stopped.

'There are almost five of us,' Stella pondered.

'Four, plus Luca,' Dahlia confirmed.

'It'd be fun to put on a play!' Poppy said. 'We've never done anything like that before.' Poppy's always willing to try out new and crazy things.

'Yeah, we could do it,' Dahlia said.

Everyone turned to look at Stella. I held my breath. I didn't want to let on how tense I was. I tried to give Stella a pleading look, even though I hadn't actually asked her anything. We usually ask Stella's opinion before doing stuff, though.

For just a moment, Stella seemed to be daydreaming. Then she focused her eyes and looked back in my direction. 'It's a terrific idea.'

I was just about ready to burst with happiness.

'Do you … Do you really mean it?' I asked. I was terrified they might change their minds.

'Definitely,' Stella replied.

I couldn't contain my joy. 'Thankyouthank-youthankyou!!!'

First I hugged Stella, then Poppy and Dahlia. They were laughing, but that didn't matter. I was so happy!

Now that a little time has passed, I'm still so happy I can't keep my hat on.

Actually, I'm a little scared too. I just realised that in order to get my idea off the ground, we're gonna have to do a lot of work, work, and more work. I'm not even sure if we'll be able to do everything exactly as I imagined. But I'm determined. I intend to make sure the play turns out perfectly.

But check this out: We're really going to put on a play! Build a stage, sew costumes, rehearse our lines, play all the characters! Nothing could make me happier.

My friends are simply amazing. ♡

Date: ....SATURDAY........

Dear Diary,

Today was a rainy day, so nothing much happened. I had been planning to try and paint another sunrise, but the sky was so grey I gave up and went back to bed. I didn't get up for several more hours, and after pondering for a few minutes I decided to organise my box of hats. Now it's so late in the day there's not much use in starting a new project. So I thought I'd write something here to pass the time.

I could tell you a little about my home. I live in a big treehouse with plenty of space to paint and hang out. My house is a little shabby, but that makes it feel homey. Sometimes I meet up with everybody at the top of the tree and drink some coffee. The cappuccinos are the best on the whole island – you should try one! (I hope you don't mind these coffee-cup stains.)

~~I just realised it's really late and I'm drinking coffee! Now I won't be able to get to sleep ... It's your own fault, Willow!~~

There's a swing outdoors that I go on whenever I'm worried about something. There's nothing more relaxing than going on a swing. And if swinging doesn't help ... well, that means there's no quick fix. Only real action will solve the problem.

~~I remember the time when Stella didn't talk to me for a whole day and I thought I had done something wrong. But then, when I worked up the courage to find out what was going on, it turned out Stella had a really sore throat and she thought Poppy had explained the situation to me.~~ Fortunately, most of my problems are the kind that disappear in a second, as soon as I stop thinking about them.

It's still raining. I just love being home alone and listening to the patter of raindrops.

LATER

Just as I feared: I can't sleep! I guess I'll write a little more.

I have always loved art. I've never told anybody this, but someday I'd like to become a painter or writer. The feeling I get when I create a painting or poem ... I just can't describe it ♡!! Well, maybe if I become a writer someday, then I'll be able to. Not now. Art just makes me so happy. Sometimes I get so excited I can't hide my feelings. That's what happened recently, when I got the brilliant idea to write my play. When I finished it, I was jumping and bouncing around and laughing so much that my friends gave me some funny looks. Well, these days they're pretty much used to my 'enthusiasm'. ☺

I love trees, too. I love their shapes, colours, smells, the way they feel. The sighing, swishing, rustling, and all the other sounds they make. I could watch them all day long and not get even the tiniest bit bored.

Now I have a bit of a confession to make. Sometimes, if I'm feeling a little bit down or just in a sensitive mood, I'll go into the forest and talk to the trees. I tell them all my secrets, and they never judge me. Sometimes I just encourage the trees to grow big and strong. I think they really like that. Anyway, the trees I visit regularly have been spared by the pigs!

Now, I'm not claiming that's because of me, but my visits don't seem to do them any harm. Before I leave, I sometimes hug them.

Does that make me sound a little ditzy? I hope not. But maybe I can explain it another way: Trees are my home. And without a home, I would have nothing.

Now do you see what I mean?

Date: MONDAY

Dear Diary,

Yesterday everybody read my play. ~~Eek!~~ I was super-nervous, but the girls seemed to like the story. The play is about a princess who stands her ground against the pigs and saves the forest where she lives. She's a true heroine! ~~Sort of the kind I'd like to be someday.~~ Not some glossy cover girl, but a really smart character with a heart, who doesn't let her fears prevent her from achieving great things.

Today we had our first rehearsal. Everybody was excited. We only had one problem: none of us knows how to put on a play or how you're supposed to rehearse. I have some idea of how I want it to look when it's finished. I know a lot about plays and other theatre stuff. I've read a lot about them. I know how that stuff works IN THEORY. In practical terms, all I know is that something happens between the script and the final performance, but what that something is, ~~I don't have a clue~~ we'll just have to figure out through trial and error.

So it came as a big shock when Stella started out by looking at me and saying, 'Willow, you'll have to be the director.'

'Me?' I asked in astonishment.

'It's your play,' Stella replied. 'And you're the one who knows the most about the theatre.'

That was definitely true, and for a moment I was enthusiastic about the responsibility I'd been given. But then I realised who I was going to be directing, and suddenly I wasn't so confident anymore.

I gulped. I tried to assume an expression that commanded respect. 'So, next we could ...' I lost my courage mid-sentence. '... Maybe choose actors for all the parts?'

'Here's what we'll do,' Stella said. 'Who do you guys think should play the leading role?' Stella stepped into the centre of the room, her head held high.

'YOU, of course!' Poppy exclaimed. Dahlia nodded behind her.

'What do you think?' Stella asked me.

'I guess it's agreed,' I mumbled.

Then we assigned the rest of the parts. I got a pretty important role: I would be the princess's lady-in-waiting. Poppy, Dahlia and Luca got the next most important parts.

I took a deep breath and tried to be firm. 'Today, we can still read from the scripts, but I hope you'll know your lines by heart tomorrow,' I said.

I'm afraid my expression didn't have the effect I wanted, because everybody looked at me like I was a little bit nuts.

'You didn't say we'd have to rehearse without a script,' Dahlia said after a pause.

'I didn't realise I'd need to spell that out! Isn't it obvious?'

'Wait a minute,' Poppy said. 'Do you mean I have to memorise all my character's lines, word for word? BY TOMORROW?'

'You have maybe eight lines,' I sighed. In fact, I knew it was exactly eight, but Poppy is the kind of bird who doesn't appreciate exactness. It's usually better to seem as if you don't know exactly what you're talking about. For some reason, it makes more of an impression on her.

'Well, I'm not used to thinking very precisely about what I say,' she said defensively.

'Yeah, and it shows.'

'HEY!'

'Shouldn't we get down to business?' Stella asked.

The rest of the rehearsal didn't go much better, so I'm not going to write anything about it. I felt small, but I resisted the urge to hide under my hat. Stella had the situation more under control than I did, even though I was supposed to be the one who was in charge of the others. ARGH! I can't shake off the feeling that the rehearsal was a failure. ~~I was a failure.~~

Now I realise I'm starting to feel sad, Diary. The thing is, when I wrote that play, I imagined myself in the leading role. It's kind of silly, but that's what I thought. Of course, I understand why everybody thought Stella was the right choice.

Even so, I just stood there without saying anything. I couldn't open my beak. Would the others have considered me a realistic choice? Hardly. Nobody suggested anyone other than Stella. She's exactly like the princess in the play.

It was only our first rehearsal. They're my friends. They'll listen to me.

I hope.

Date: TUESDAY

Oh, dear Diary,

Something terrible has happened. My favourite hat is missing. I repeat, MY FAVOURITE HAT IS MISSING!

Here are the details, in case you might have seen it:

MISSING: Hat
COLORS: Yellow and orange
SIZE: Medium
CONDITION: Used lovingly for approximately five years

REWARD!

Fortunately, I do have other hats. Without a hat, I'd feel naked. Half of my identity would be missing. Half of my head, too, or at least that's what it feels like when I take off my hat. I'm not used to having my head subjected to the forces of nature.

Over the years, I've developed a way of storing various things in my hat, such as pens, paintbrushes, and, in emergencies, even pretzels and cupcakes. That refers to situations that only arise if your friends are birds who haven't completely adopted the notion of sharing equally.

A hat will make anyone cool. I've built my whole style around it. Without a hat, I have no style.

I'm gonna tell you a secret: I have a suspect in mind. Her name starts with P and ends with Y. And just in case that's not clear (obviously I don't doubt your intellectual powers, Diary, but we all have our off days), the letters in the middle are O, P, and P.

At this point it might be good to point out that the bird I mentioned (the one whose name begins with P) and my hat have some history. My beloved hats have ended up in the claws of that bird of prey before. This tragic tale goes all the way back to the days when we were just little chicks. In those days, Poppy always wanted to be the centre of attention. She's never exactly been the most tactful or considerate bird, either, and thinking back, nothing's changed since our chickhood. She figured out that the best way to get my undivided attention was to take my hat and keep it out of my reach for as long as possible.

I thought Poppy had left her hat-bullying days behind. But no. Nobody understands how great hats are. And some will take advantage of your devotion to hats.

Have no fear, my dear hat. I'll rescue you!

Date: WEDNESDAY

Dear Diary,

A playwright writes the script. A costume designer designs and makes costumes. It's clear what a set designer and lighting designer do. Everybody knows what actors do. But what does a director actually do? Shout at everybody else during rehearsals?

Do you know, Diary?

I just don't have a clue.

We had another rehearsal today.

'Dahlia, could you try to show a little more life in your facial expressions?' I asked. Actually, I thought of ordering her rather than asking, but that would have been rude. I wanted to start by rehearsing the scene that I thought needed the most work. And how right I was!

'But this is how I always look at you guys,' Dahlia said defensively.

That was true, but it didn't make her acting any better.

I decided to focus on Poppy. 'Poppy, turn and face left. No, that's your right. Left. And now say your line.'

'I haven't memorised it yet.'

'Well, read it from the script then.'

'I lost it.'

I sighed. 'All right, let's stop for today.'

'Yay! Man, I am HUNGRY.' Poppy hopped down off the stage.

I was irritated.

'How come you look so crabby?' Poppy asked.

She was obviously trying to annoy me. 'I know it was you who took my hat,' I said. Or more precisely, it slipped out and sounded even nastier than I intended.

'What on earth are you talking about?'

When I didn't reply, Poppy just shrugged and went out, whistling a tune. She didn't let anything slip!

~~And why would she?~~

Let's face the facts. I'm not a born director. Stella is. But with Stella playing the leading role and Dahlia in charge of the set and lighting, there's no one but me. Of course, there's Poppy, but as long as I'm telling the truth here, I've got to say we'll be lucky if she manages to learn those eight lines. If you tell her to organise a great party, generate as much noise and chaos or steal somebody's favourite hat (grr!), it's guaranteed to turn out great. Anything else, and it's a different story.

Anyway, I'm the only one who knows the script inside-out and understands the play's fundamental message. I don't think the others have got far enough to grasp the big issues it deals with. It's not just a play. It's our lives!

From now on, I've got to be more assertive, louder, and more organised! I should also start demanding more from my friends, otherwise the play won't turn out the way I want it to. You can do it, Willow!!

Date: THURSDAY

Dear Diary,

We've been working hard the last couple of days. I thought it would help our acting to have our costumes ready while we're still rehearsing. My thinking is, if our appearance on the outside matches the internal world of our characters, the right expressions will just come about on their own.

I found that gimmick in one of my books. I hope it'll work. I don't actually know what I'll do if this play doesn't come together!

We've set up a base in our tree's common area. Dahlia's come up with some incredible ways of using the materials we have, and we've got our first outfits finished. We tried them on Poppy and Stella.

And then something happened that I'd better tell you about.

'This looks really good,' Stella said as she looked at herself in the mirror.

'Yeah! Even Gale would approve of that outfit. Except Gale would never agree to wear anything that was made out of rubbish,' Poppy said.

Stella's expression changed. She tried to hide it, but I could see how sad she was at the mention of Gale's name. Gale used to be Stella's best friend, you see. They were inseparable, or at least that's what we all thought.

At some point, Gale started to change. At first, she just got more arrogant and would always be checking herself out in the mirror. Clearly, we weren't good enough for her. Then Gale left us. Now she thinks she's a princess, and I don't mean just in her attitude. None of us knows what got into her. ~~Or had she always been that snooty, and we just didn't realise it?~~

Stella was powerless to do anything about it, and I think it affected her the most. I think she believes Gale wouldn't have turned out the way she did if only Stella could have given her enough help and support. Stella blames herself.

We don't know for certain what Gale's been up to since she left. All we know is that she bosses the pigs around, and they do whatever she tells them to. She lives on the other side of the island, and we don't go there unless we absolutely have to. Maybe we should keep a closer eye on her, but right now none of us feels like it. I used to paint a new group portrait of us every year, but

since Gale left I haven't done one. I also hid all of my old paintings.

So you see, Diary, things are pretty bad.

In any case, I think Gale's situation is a lot worse than ours. We've got each other. She doesn't have anybody but the pigs. She must feel very lonely!

But there's no use dwelling on the past. I ought to focus on the here and now. Tomorrow I get to try on my own dress! I can't wait!

LATER THAT DAY

I spent some time thinking about my friends today. First of all: Poppy still hasn't given me my hat back. She's a little riddle. On the outside she gives the impression that what you see is what you get, but I know she's really not that straightforward. She's blunt and loud and can be kind of inconsiderate sometimes – at least I think so, even though I know she doesn't really mean to be. I think she's just trying to have fun most of the time.

What can we learn from this? It's tough to be funny. That's why I avoided writing a comedy and stuck to drama.

Out of the four and a half of us, the one I identify with most is Dahlia. Both of us can get so wrapped up in our own projects that the rest of the world disappears. I don't think Stella and Poppy really understand that. They both have plenty of things they like to do, but they don't have the same passion.

Maybe they're so talented they don't need to try as hard. Oh wait, I think Dahlia's really talented. She might even be the most gifted of all of us. She can use her talents to achieve something really important. For some reason, I've never been jealous of her. I've never wanted to be like her, even though she's totally awesome. Even little things interest Dahlia and make her happy. That's a skill I ought to learn! Also on the list: snorkeling, saying 'no,' and flipping pancakes.

I'm never completely satisfied with my art. Dahlia doesn't seem to have that problem. She never seems disappointed, even though her experiments usually go wrong. Once she told me it's impossible for an experiment to go wrong. When she finds out something doesn't work, that's a success in itself. No matter how much I try to think that way about what I do, it never seems to work!

So maybe I am a little jealous of Dahlia after all. But Stella? There aren't too many days when

I wouldn't trade places with her in the blink of an eye.

I wonder if Stella ever has thoughts like this. Or Poppy? Hard to imagine. But maybe I'm wrong. Maybe they do think I have it easier than them. That's a weird thought.

What am I saying here? I don't really think my life is bad at all. Everything's fine!!!

Sometimes I just don't remember that. Fortunately, though, you don't complain, Diary. You don't judge me at all, at least not too quickly. I admit you might get a very strange impression of me from the entries I've written here.

Oh yeah, I almost forgot to mention: We decided the play is going to be performed a week and a half from now, on Monday. That's ten days from today! TEN DAYS!!! We don't have much time at all. I'm worried things won't be ready in time, but I'm determined. This is my play. I'm going to do everything I can to make it as good as it can be!

Date: FRIDAY

Dear Diary,

We've moved from our tree to the theatre. Most of the costumes are finished, and now it's time for the set. I drew a picture of how I want the stage to look, and it's Dahlia's job to come up with a way to do it. We've been sawing, nailing and painting. Making costumes requires attention to detail, while building the set takes strength and calm nerves. It's a lot harder work than I imagined! A few times I've even thought we should drop some of the more difficult items (for example, maybe the princess could hide behind a tree instead of climbing up it). So far, though, I've stuck to my original vision.

Today we were really busy. Everybody had their own job to do, and everything was going well. A little too well, as it turned out.

'Where's Luca?' Dahlia suddenly asked.

At this point I should mention that Luca has actually been with us at all of our rehearsals and all the time we've been sewing and building. He's as excited about everything as the rest of us. The only problem is that when he gets excited, he starts moving around really fast. When you combine that with the fact that we girls always have too much to do, it's a miracle we hadn't lost him before now.

We all peered around, looking for Luca but we couldn't find him anywhere.

'Let's split up,' Stella said. So that's what we did. It definitely wasn't the first time Luca had managed to slip away somewhere, but this time I was more worried than ever before. As if I felt more responsible this time, now that I was the director of the play.

'Luca!' I shouted. No reply.

I dashed back and forth. I don't even know how much time passed.

Just as I was starting to think we'd lost him for good, I heard Stella's voice calling, 'Hey, everybody! I found him!'

~~I was so relieved I could have cried.~~ If I'm honest, I think I shed a few tears, but I managed to compose myself before I got back to the others. Luca seemed to be his old self. In fact, he appeared even more enthusiastic than usual, and I can only imagine what an exciting adventure his escapade must have been. I wasn't sure if he even understood how much we were panicking. Probably not. If he had understood, he would have known not to cause us so much worry.

I don't know what I would do if anything happened to Luca. I'm sure it would be too much to bear. He still doesn't understand what a dangerous place the world is.

LATER THAT DAY

I can't get to sleep. Luca's disappearance worked me up into such a frenzy, I can't really deal with it.

I've been thinking about the play. In fact, I haven't just been thinking. I've actually been rehearsing all my lines in front of the mirror. Sometimes when I can't get to sleep, I'll get up and repeat my lines out loud on my swing. I don't have all that many lines, but I'm still afraid I might forget them.

So, what else? Poppy is still reading from her script in rehearsals. Stella doesn't always remember everything either, but she fills in with her own lines. True, that's better than what Poppy does, but it still annoys me sometimes. If

I wanted my heroine to say, 'Game on!' instead of 'Let battle commence!' I would have written that!

Stella always gets everything. Everything's always so easy for her. She has no idea what it's like to be ordinary. When nobody notices you or pays attention to you. When nothing goes the way you want it to. Maybe if somebody else were in the spotlight besides her for once, she might understand how things are for the rest of us. Or, at least, for me. Poppy has barely noticed whether she's in the leading role or a supporting part. And Dahlia seems pretty happy, too. Maybe I'm the only one who wishes things were different.

What does that say about me?

Maybe I'm just selfish. I wonder if I'm longing for attention. Or maybe I'm just not brave enough. The others have gotten what they wanted, so why can't I?

What is it that I really want?

Don't get me wrong, Diary. Stella's my friend. Maybe even my best friend. ~~Sometimes I wonder if Stella really is as perfect as she seems.~~

~~Would I find it easier to like Stella if she weren't so pretty?~~

I have to admit, Stella's not bad at all in the part of the princess. In fact, she's brilliant. ~~Way better than I would be~~. I know I should be happy about that, but sometimes it's hard. She's my friend.

Sometimes I'm just too envious of her. That's not her fault – it's mine! I ought be a better bird, not as selfish as I am now … I wish I could talk to somebody about this, but I'm afraid nobody would understand. Poppy might laugh. Dahlia would just feel awkward. And Stella … Stella's the one I would normally go and talk to. But now I don't know. Could I admit I'm envious of her? What would she think of me after that?

What if she didn't want to be my friend anymore?

Now I feel like I want to cry. I want to do everything right, but what if I can't?!? I try so hard, but then things just go wrong. Maybe I should just give up!

Date: SATURDAY

Dear Diary,

Dahlia has come up with a harebrained idea. You could call it: 'Use all your time trying to decide how to do something, without actually getting around to doing it.'

Is Dahlia losing her mind? How come she's behaving like this? We don't care whether all of her calculations are as neatly presented as they could be. I repeat: Nobody is interested in numbers on a piece of paper, as long as they stay on paper! We have no time to waste, but it seems to me that all she's doing is wasting time.

We don't have time. I constantly try to remind them about that, but why does it seem like nobody's listening to me? Like just now: I told Dahlia she needed to get the set finished for tomorrow, and do you know what Poppy said? 'Don't sweat it!'

Don't sweat it?!?

Poppy is definitely not helping matters. She'd rather cackle at her own dumb jokes than actually do anything.

Okay, so some of her jokes are pretty good in normal circumstances, but I simply can't laugh now, at least not openly. I need to concentrate on directing.

The only one who's doing her fair share is Stella, but she has so many lines to learn, it's stretching her to the limit. Besides, she's still taking a lot of freedoms with her lines. Every time I try to drop a hint about that, she gives such a good reason for doing what she did, I get even more irritated than before. Does she think I didn't consider each and every line as carefully as I could?

And then, of course, there's Luca. We're under huge pressure, and then that little pain goes and messes something up. All of us almost had a heart attack today when he crawled underneath a huge pile of fabrics.

And my hat ... That goes without saying. Poppy still hasn't confessed. I tried to give her the silent treatment, but then I felt so bad I couldn't keep it up and apologised to her.

I actually apologised to her, even though I know she took my hat! What is wrong with me?!

Gotta go now – I'll tell you more tomorrow.

Date: SUNDAY

Dear Diary,

I woke up in the middle of the night. The sky was dark, and I could make out a few stars. It took me a moment to realise why I'd woken up.

A noise. It came from somewhere far away, and at first I almost thought I was just hearing things. But no.

A crash. And then another.

I started to cry. I knew what those noises meant. I'd heard them before. It was the sound of falling trees. One, two, three ... so many I couldn't count them through my tears. The pigs had started destroying the forest again!

I don't know how long I'd been crying when someone appeared in my room. Stella gave me a hug and rocked me gently.

She said, 'There, there, don't worry.' She said a lot of other things, too, but I didn't hear them because I was crying. So it didn't matter what she said, because we both knew her words wouldn't change what had happened. No matter how brave Stella is, this was something she couldn't do anything about. She couldn't stop the pigs from wrecking stuff any more than I could.

The sound of trees falling is the most horrible sound in the entire world. It breaks my heart.

LATER

Dear Diary,

Last night made me so upset, I've been down in the dumps all day. We tried to pretend everything was OK, but I could see in my friends' eyes that they'd heard what happened during the night too. We all kept our beaks tightly shut. I'm writing this while my friends are next door, working on the props and costumes. We're continuing with our jobs we didn't finish yesterday. Stella's using way too much force to hammer some boards together. Poppy hasn't cracked any of her usual jokes and hasn't picked up her drumsticks.

I'm having a hard time concentrating. I can't help but think that, right now, the pigs are knocking down trees and shrubs. The whole time we've been rehearsing our play, the pigs have been wrecking the island, and we didn't notice a thing.

It's all Gale's fault! She's giving orders to the pigs. The pigs don't act on their own – they're not smart enough. We don't know why Gale is doing all this. Is she really evil? If only we knew why, we could stop her.

At some point I'm sure we'll discover the destruction the pigs have caused this time. But not today, and not tomorrow either. Maybe not even next week. Stella always says we should avoid bumping into the pigs, but I know there are other reasons, too. A forest that's just been cut down is one of the saddest sights imaginable. A reminder that we're already too late to do anything.

The worst thing is, we have no way of knowing how long this is going to last. The pigs might strike again tomorrow! They might continue until there's nothing left on the island. What will we do if they come closer to our home? Will we move somewhere else, or just hope they leave us alone? I don't have any answers, and I'm worried Stella doesn't either.

Still, life has to go on. But part of me wonders what use this play is when such terrible things are going on.

But maybe the purpose of the play is to give us something else to think about. Helping us to take comfort in each other and find joy in simple things. Sometimes I forget the play isn't real: I think Stella really is a good princess who can clobber the pigs. I allow myself to imagine we've really achieved something. That brings me back to reality with an even bigger jolt. But it's no use worrying. We've got to find a way.

You might think I'm a real treehugger, but the truth is, if there were more ~~treehuggers~~ friends of the environment, things would be a whole lot better. Imagine what would happen if the pigs suddenly became environmentalists and replanted every single tree they've cut down on this island. That'd be amazing!

I'm afraid this island won't be the place it used to be for much longer. And at some point it won't even exist at all. Some people might say that wouldn't bother them, but I bet they'd be mad if their home was destroyed. And not just their first home, but the next one and then the next. We have to understand that this might never end. Not if we just sit here and wait. ☹

Trees are the island's lungs. The fewer trees we have, the less oxygen we'll have. We won't appreciate being able to breathe until there's no more air. I know this from experience – once I almost drowned underneath a waterfall. Sorry, Diary, but that was so awful I don't even want to talk about it with you. The memory of it still hurts. What I can say is that whenever life feels lousy, I remember that time and I'm instantly thankful to be alive.

LATER THAT DAY

Just as we were rehearsing the play, something strange happened. Stella and I were practising our first scene together, when Stella suddenly said, 'Sorry about that.'

'About what?' I asked. I was totally confused. She hadn't done a single thing wrong during the whole rehearsal.

'The pigs. About the fact I'm not like the princess in the play.' She tossed the sword, which is part of her costume, to the ground. 'I've been thinking all day long about what I could do to make it stop. And I couldn't come up with anything.' She looked really furious.

I blinked. Stella looked serious. I hadn't realised she felt guilty. I cleared my throat. 'I don't imagine there's anything you can do. Neither can I. Even so, this island is our home.

The pigs' reign of destruction is harming all of us. Including you.'

Stella looked at me for a long time without saying anything. Just then, Poppy showed up. 'Hey, check it out! I'm a PIG!'

That she was. She was wearing a green pig suit and a pig snout.

A moment before then, I would have been sure I wouldn't laugh at anything connected with the pigs, but Poppy looked so dumb, I didn't have any choice. I just lost it. Stella and I laughed ourselves silly as Poppy started oinking and making faces at us. No more doom and gloom! I've gotta say, Poppy's acting was terrific. 😄

Date: MONDAY

Dear Diary,

Sometimes I feel like I'm too sensitive. I feel things too strongly. It would be a lot easier if I felt things less. But then again, feelings are what make life so amazing!

When I'm happy, I'm really, really happy.

I feel like shouting and can't sit still. That happens when I finish a painting I've been working on for a long time, or when I suddenly get a great idea. As if somebody else were guiding my paintbrush for me. I don't think about anything. I just do. Sometimes it just happens out of the blue, if the weather's nice or the clouds make pretty shapes or for no reason at all.

Sometimes I think I care too much. Sometimes that's painful.

But. At least I can say that I have a lot more in my life than the average bird my age. I don't just live one life. I've got all the characters in my play, together and separately! All those stories seem true to me, in a way.

Some people might say I love art because I don't achieve enough myself, and I'm trying to live through others. But isn't that what we all do? Isn't it more cowardly to try to act like you don't care about anything? I think that's a really sad, lonely life. I can't cut myself off from this world and the amazing things in it, and I don't want to. I'm a part of all of it, part of all of us. ♡

Date: TUESDAY

Dear Diary,

Our rehearsal today was a total flop! Nobody could concentrate. ~~Not even me.~~ Here's just one example of what I had to put up with today.

'Poppy! You're standing in front of Stella again,' I said for about the millionth time. 'Nobody in the audience can see Stella.'

'So?' Poppy asked.

'The princess is the main character in the story! The audience will want to see her!'

'How am I supposed to know that?'

I sighed. Finally, Poppy agreed to move over towards stage right. Stella had just opened her beak and said 'I –' when the curtain came down right in the middle of everything.

'What did you do that for, Dahlia?' I asked.

Dahlia's head poked out from the side of the stage. 'Isn't this where the play ends?' she asked.

'No,' Stella shouted from underneath the curtain, which had landed right on her head!

What can I say, Diary? It really looks like my play is going to be a disaster. We're all starting to get worn out.

But we don't have any other choice. The show must go on! Tomorrow's another day! I'm going to bed now. Good night, Diary!

Date: WEDNESDAY

Dear Diary,

Sometimes I think I'd be a really bad actress. I'm sure everyone would see right through me. I'm not really that talented. But I want it more than anybody else! I'm ready to do anything, Diary, anything to realise my dream. ~~If my friends don't believe me~~... I don't think anybody knows just how important art is to me.

Sometimes I just wish I could show everybody how fragile I really am. ~~I wish I didn't need to keep anything secret.~~ But maybe we all have to conceal things from ourselves. Maybe we can't be totally honest, so instead we just adapt to other people's expectations of us. Or maybe we set our own expectations and then blame other people.

But still, sometimes I feel like I need to hide my true self. I try to tell the others what excites me, but my ideas never seem as important to them as they do to me. Not that they should.

But.

Sometimes it makes me feel isolated. Like nobody really understands. I don't know why I haven't told my friends about my dreams. Maybe I'm just scared they wouldn't take them seriously enough.

Well, I don't really think my friends would laugh at me or anything like that. But I'd want them to be encouraging, and if they weren't, that would be a lot worse than if they had never found out about the whole thing. I don't know if I could trust them afterwards.

So it's better they don't know. That way I can imagine anything is possible. Their opinions are so important to me. And why wouldn't they be? They're smart and pretty and braver than me. If they don't believe in my abilities, I won't have any opportunities. And isn't it a little bit like how your dreams vanish if you talk about them too much? Maybe I'm superstitious, but that's what I think.

Sometimes I realise how hopeless my dreams are. I love Golden Island, but this place is so small. There aren't any opportunities here to become a great artist or writer. Not even an actress or theatre director. Sometimes I wonder whether it makes any sense to put on a play just for ourselves. Look at all this wasted effort when we don't have an audience! There's nobody we could invite. The pigs?

~~Maybe there's no point to the things I want after all.~~ Why do I have the feeling this project is slipping out of my hands? ~~Who am I trying to kid?~~

This play is my dream. Mine! How come the others won't let it turn out the way I want?

Date: THURSDAY

ODE TO A HAT

OH HAT OF MINE,
SO WARM AND DEAR
I'D DO ANYTHING
TO HAVE YOU HERE
BUT POPPY IS DUMB
AND WE WILL BECOME
THE GROUP THAT CAN'T EVEN GET
THIS PLAY READY!!!

Just FYI, Diary: if anybody ever reads this, I will die of embarrassment.

Date: FRIDAY

Dear Diary,

Yesterday something big happened. I mean, BIG. I'm still a little confused about what happened, so I'll see if I can get it to make sense here.

I'll try.

Diary, you might have been able to tell from my previous entries that I've been a little stressed and unhappy at how my play has been going. I didn't realise how frustrated I had become.

It all started when somebody pulled my hat down over my eyes.

'Stop fooling around,' I said. 'We're not five-year-olds anymore.'

'No, but this is still fun!' I heard Poppy's voice say.

'I don't think it's ever been fun,' I grumbled as I pulled my hat off. Poppy didn't hear, though.

Or if she did, she didn't react. Poppy is one of those birds who never takes things seriously, either the things she says or what others say.

'We've got a lot of work ahead of us today,' I said, placing my hat back on my head.

'You've been saying that all week,' Poppy remarked.

'Yeah, because we're behind schedule.'

'What schedule?'

'The play's schedule.'

'You mean the schedule you came up with yourself.'

'Which we all decided on together,' I said patiently.

'I think we've been rehearsing a little too much,' Poppy said. Dahlia nodded beside her, and I was annoyed to see Stella didn't disagree.

'We're still not ready,' I tried to explain. 'Some scenes are still really rough.'

'What difference does it make, when there's nobody watching?'

'It does make a difference,' I said. I hoped nobody would notice how thin my voice sounded. 'We have to do our best, whether we have an audience or not. It's hard to explain. We owe it to ourselves! And to this island, and its trees.'

Poppy started to giggle. That was the final straw.

I lost my temper. Really blew my top.

Me!

I yelled at the top of my voice. 'This is not a joke! Do you realise how long I've been dreaming of this play? Do you have any idea how long it took me to write it?!' And once I'd got started, there was no stopping me. 'Have any of you stopped to think what this play is about? Or aren't you interested? The pigs are really, truly destroying our island! AND YOU GUYS ARE JUST MUCKING AROUND AND SPOILING EVERYTHING!!!'

I gasped for breath. Only when I felt my pulse returning to normal did I notice that my friends were staring at me.

They stared at me for a loooooong tiiiiiiiime.

Stella was the first one to open her beak. 'I'm sorry you feel that we haven't been taking the play seriously enough. I don't think any of us did it on purpose. Right, Poppy?'

'That's right,' Poppy said in an embarrassed voice. 'You know I like to joke about everything. That's just how I am. It doesn't mean anything.' I had never seen her so serious. 'Sorry.'

'And I'm sorry I didn't let you direct, and just started giving out orders on your behalf,' Stella said.

So she *had* noticed!

'Sorry I haven't stuck to the schedule. This has been such a technically challenging project,' Dahlia said.

Even Luca peeped something. His face was so sad I immediately regretted my outburst. I went over to him and gave him a hug.

'No, I'm sorry,' I said. 'I should have told you all how I was feeling. And I should have believed you, Poppy, when you said you didn't take my hat. I should have trusted all of you more. Even if you're not doing everything exactly the way I want, that doesn't mean the end result won't be just as good, or even better.'

Stella smiled. 'We're all different, and that's our strength. We complete one another. Sometimes that means that we might get in each other's way, but so what? We can argue because we trust each other.'

'Group hug?' I asked tentatively.

And before I knew it, I was covered in hugs from every direction. Stella, Dahlia, and Poppy gave me a big squeeze, and Luca hopped and bounced up against me. I was so touched that if they hadn't been hugging me so tightly I couldn't breathe, I would have started crying. Why on earth did I doubt my friends? They're the best!

'OK, that's enough!' Poppy said. 'You said we still need to rehearse.'

And so we did. Everything went really well, and even Poppy remembered her lines! ~~Well, not exactly, but almost.~~ We're a fantastic team.

~~For the first time in my life I dared to get mad, and you know what, Diary? It felt good.~~ I definitely don't plan to yell at my friends again anytime soon.

LATER

I found my hat. It had slid out of my hat-box and landed between the dresser and the wall. It must have happened when I was organising my box of hats. So it had nothing to do with Poppy. Now I feel a little ashamed. Although Poppy is still Hat Enemy No. 1. 😉

Date: SUNDAY

Dear Diary,

I didn't have time to write yesterday. We're so busy getting everything ready. Today we had our dress rehearsal. Poppy forgot some of her lines, and I was so nervous I was stuttering.

I'm so terrified, Diary. What if everything goes wrong tomorrow? What if I can't say my lines? Or I fall down? Or something even worse happens – something I haven't even had time to be afraid of? ☹

Date: MONDAY (THE GRAND PREMIERE!)

Dear Diary,

I'm so nervous, I'm going to try and unload my nerves onto you.

I'll describe our awesome theatre for you. Dahlia and I painted two different backdrops that are switched around during the interval. Dahlia also came up with a great system that makes it super-easy to change the sets and backdrops.

Stella has five costumes, Poppy and I each have two, and Dahlia and Luca each have one. Yep, Luca's in the play, too. ~~You'll see for yourself. Well, not exactly *see*, but I'll try to describe everything as vividly as I can so you can imagine it in your mind's eye just the way it happened.~~

~~Even though you don't have eyes.~~ I'm trying to give as detailed a description as I can so I'll always be able to return to this moment in later years.

~~Except, of course, if everything goes wrong, in which case I'm probably better off sticking with a brief list of things.~~

I can feel that I'm starting to panic again about tonight, so I'll go back to writing about the set design and what's backstage. So Dahlia has just one costume. Her part in the actual play is pretty small, but that's how she wanted it. Her main role is working behind the scenes and making sure all the technical stuff works. She's the only one who even knows what a winch and cables are. All those designs and calculations ...

well, Diary, it looks like I was too harsh when I complained that Dahlia wasn't getting anything done. In fact, she got a WHOLE LOT done.

LATER THAT DAY

It's the interval. So far, everything's going well. I didn't sleep a wink last night, but I've got so much adrenaline in me, I don't even feel tired. Gotta go now –

ACT 2 IS ABOUT
TO START!

Date: WEDNESDAY

Dear Diary,

What an amazing day it was! We partied late into the night.

But let me backtrack a little. I'm sure you want to hear how everything went and how the play turned out.

I'll start right before the play began. Since we didn't have an audience, we agreed we'd sit in the seats whenever we weren't on stage ourselves. I was in the first scene.

I was standing behind the curtain and could hear my own pulse. My heart was pounding so hard, I was afraid it would burst out of my chest. I knew that only Poppy and Luca were sitting in the audience, because Stella was also in the first scene and Dahlia was backstage making sure everything worked the way it should.

I looked to the right, where Stella stood and waited. She appeared calm. She was wearing a red dress. Right then, I wasn't jealous of her at all – I looked good myself. I'd made myself a hat that not only covered my whole head, but also totally matched the style of my character as a lady-in-waiting. My character might not be a princess like Stella's character, but she was just as important.

'Everybody ready?' Dahlia asked, clearing her throat. She was standing near the crank that raised the curtain.

Stella looked at me. She gave a little smile and nodded bravely. 'Yep,' she said. 'Game on!'

Stella trusted me! Maybe I should trust myself, too.

Dahlia started cranking the curtain up. The lights were bright and made me squint. I couldn't really see the audience. There could have been two birds or two hundred out there. I glanced down and gave a look that I'd been practising in front of the mirror.

The play began.

Stella appeared next to me. 'What's the matter, Therese?'

And guess what, Diary? Something strange happened just then. I was no longer nervous at all. I forgot I was on stage. I was immersed in my role. I was no longer Willow – I was Therese, the grief-stricken lady-in-waiting, who had witnessed the destruction caused by the pigs with her own eyes.

'Oh, your highness, what dreadful things are concealed in this world! How beauty can be turned into ugliness in the blink of an eye.'

'What do you mean, my dear Therese?'

'The forest, your highness ...'

'Did you go into the forest on your own?' the princess asked.

'Yes,' I replied.

'Isn't that forbidden?'

'Yes indeed, your highness, but I had to see it with my own eyes. And now I have seen it.'

Diary, I can't describe everything to you, because I don't really remember. After the first scene, I went out into the audience and sat down next to Poppy.

'How does it look?' I whispered.

'Awesome!'

The play continued. On stage I had lost myself in my role, and once I was in the audience, I got totally absorbed in the story. The princess decided to disguise herself as a lady-in-waiting and venture into the forest. She expressed all the terror and was really frantic. She had a long monologue, in which her sadness turned to anger and then determination. She wasn't going to let the pigs destroy the forest anymore.

Stella was amazing. She had changed a few of her lines and left pauses in places where I hadn't planned them, but it made her performance even better.

'You know, even though I've read this play UMPTEEN times, I'm still excited to find out what happens next,' Poppy whispered.

'I know. Aren't you supposed to be on-stage?'

'Oops!' Poppy leaped up and raced onto the stage. She reached her spot just in time to say her first line.

On stage, the princess made her decision: she would put on some clothes she had secretly borrowed from a hunter and go back into the forest.

Diary, you're going to have to remain in suspense for a little bit, because I'm taking a little break from writing. I'm going to get a cup of coffee. I'll be right back!

LATER

Well then. I'm back now and ready to continue. During the interval, all of us got together upstairs, in the café that also serves as the foyer for our theatre. We drank coffee and nibbled on nuts and different sweet rolls we'd baked the day before. For most of the time, we talked about what we thought of the play so far.

'I think the princess is so incredibly brave,' Poppy began.

'I'm just afraid she's letting her heart rule her head,' Dahlia replied.

'The question of whether she's brave or foolhardy depends on how things turn out,' I said. 'If she's successful, she's a heroine. If not, she'll just look like a klutz.'

You might be wondering, Diary, why we even bothered to pretend we didn't know how the play was going to end, when we'd all read it so many times. The thing is, it's not a play without both performers and an audience. A play needs both! A performer is only a performer when somebody's watching them. Otherwise they're just playing pretend. ~~Maybe I read that in a book somewhere.~~

And for us it was the same as for anybody else who's prepared to throw themselves into a role. Just like a good book feels new every time you read it, it felt like the story changed a tiny bit each time I read it or saw it performed. I realised it wasn't my story anymore, but had taken on a life of its own.

That insight didn't make me sad – the opposite, in fact: I realised that's what theatre is all about. It's not about having one bird's ideas performed as that bird thinks they should. Every moment is new, exciting and unpredictable!

There's no harm if there's occasionally a little hiccup. Or maybe even a few.

Dahlia looked at her watch. 'The performance will continue in five minutes,' she announced.

Dahlia disappeared backstage, and the rest of us gradually went to take up our positions. Poppy had already broken into a hop.

'Luca, your turn is coming up soon,' she called out as she left.

We accompanied Luca backstage and huddled together behind the curtain.

'No need to be nervous,' Stella said. 'Just do it the way we rehearsed it.'

Luca replied with a joyful tweet. He looked like he was enjoying being the centre of attention. At least one of us wasn't showing any nerves!

I gave Luca a quick hug and went out to sit in the audience next to Poppy.

Dahlia cranked the curtain up.

Luca appeared on stage, happily chirping away. His part was to walk across the stage without stopping. He was playing a baby pig who was relaying the message that the hunter had been spotted in the forest.

Suddenly, Luca stopped in the middle of the stage. He started chirping at us and bouncing up and down. Dahlia came on stage and led him off.

'Well, that went as well as could be expected,' Poppy said next to me.

I tried to smile at her. I had tears in my eyes. Luca was so excited. Because of my play! 'Luca did just fine,' I said.

The story continued. The princess found the pigs and also happened to hear their plan to make part of the forest into a mudbath. The princess managed to get inside the pigs' castle, and finally she challenged the guard pig to a duel with wooden swords. The first to break the other's sword would win.

'If you win,' the princess said defiantly, 'you may marry me. You will get my entire realm. But if I win, you will give up the mudbath and no pig shall ever enter my land again.'

The guard pig was so smug he couldn't resist that fantastic offer. He was absolutely sure he would win. ~~That's exactly what the pigs are like!~~

I was playing the guard pig. You might think it really sucked, but when you're acting you can't think about your own likes and dislikes; you have to live the part as fully as possible. This meant that while I was being the guard pig, the pigs didn't bother me one bit! ~~It was fun to pretend to do battle against Stella. I got to work out every last bit of aggression~~. Of course, the princess won the duel, and the guard pig started to cry. I was great at pretending to cry!

'You shall never return here!' Stella – or the princess – announced to the pigs in the last scene, and the whole audience cheered. ~~That is: Poppy and Luca cheered.~~

The curtain came down, and then it went up again. Stella bowed to us, and we all cheered like crazy. Then Stella hopped down into the audience, and it was Poppy's turn to receive the applause. Next, Dahlia came out on stage and bowed along with Luca.

'Your turn, Willow!'

I went up on stage. I bowed once and then twice, as my friends didn't stop cheering.

'Oh, don't, I'm going to cry,' I said, which just made us all laugh.

I climbed down off the stage. It felt strange that the play was over. 'I think we performed pretty well,' I said. My voice sounded uncertain. I didn't want to reveal to the others how excited I was.

'Are you kidding? We did an amazing job!' Stella exclaimed.

'Definitely!'

Nobody said anything, but suddenly we all hugged one another. That's how well we all get along.

'You were fantastic,' I said to Stella.

'None of it would have happened without you, Willow,' Stella said, in an unusually serious voice.

'Thanks, you guys,' I said, with tears rolling down my cheeks.

'What are we all boo-hooing about? TIME TO PARTY!' Poppy shouted. We all cheered, and even Luca let out a piercing cheep.

We decorated our home tree with coloured lanterns, which we lit as the sun set behind the trees. Fireflies appeared as if on command, while Poppy played the drums. We danced and sang late into the night. Our home tree stood tall and reassuring, bathed in the warmth of the lights, and, at that moment, there was nowhere else in the world I'd rather be.

Date: THURSDAY

Dear Diary,

I learned a lot yesterday. I learned you don't have to aim for perfection. Who wants to be perfect, anyway? Perfect is boring. Not everything went the way we planned yesterday, but guess what, Diary? In the end, everything turned out better as a result! I had fun. It's not always easy for me to have fun, but yesterday was the most fun we've had in a long time. All that work and hassle was totally worth it!

But best of all, the others looked like they were having fun. Luca was bouncing around through the whole performance.

I also finally realised that I have no reason to be jealous of Stella. She's pretty, brave and an all-around great friend. Yesterday she said something that really made me think about things. She said, 'Nobody else is like you, Willow.'

And that's totally true, Diary! Nobody could be like me, no matter how hard they tried. I'm the only Willow there is. And I know how to be me! I have different talents than the others, and that's what makes me important.

My friends and I are kind of crazy. Every once in a while we yell at each other, but in the end, nothing can tear us apart. We're best friends!

Diary, you might still be wondering why this play was such a big deal to me. Sometimes I wonder the same thing myself. Yesterday's performance was just one play. The thing I'll always remember is that I got to share it with my friends, from beginning to end. And it turned out to be an amazing spectacle! We'll remember it for the rest of our lives.

And when I dream ... They say everybody who has a dream needs at least one bird who believes in them. I have four. I know I'm gonna succeed, Diary. I already have!

DON'T MISS THE NEXT ADVENTURE...

POPPY'S PERFECT PRANK

Date: SUNDAY

4PM

This is it! This is the best day EVER! This is going to be so TOTES FANTABULOUS that it'll go down in the *Book of Bird Records* as the prank to end all pranks. I'm so excited I can barely breathe, let alone speak. Seriously, Diary, it's going to be better than:

a) The time I swallowed twenty-seven of Dahlia's jet-propulsion sweets and whooshed around the island fourteen times in three minutes, which made Willow so dizzy she had to lie down for a day. Plus the smell was pretty spectacular, if you get my meaning. But it made ME laugh!

b) The time I put super-sticky tree sap on the swing so that Gale was stuck there for two hours. Which, if you think about it, was her own fault for trespassing. I don't know why

Willow was so annoyed. I mean, it could have been HER with her butt glued to a piece of rubber ... Though I suppose having Gale squawking outside your window might be a TEENSY-WEENSY bit annoying. But, still, worth it, right?

c) The time Stella wished we could live in a Winter Wonderland, so I spread super-slippery slime all over her treehouse to turn it into an ice rink, which it totally did! I mean, how was I to know that it would take so long to wear off that she'd be skidding around on her tail-feathers for a whole week?
d) And EVEN better than the time I hid inside Willow's hat and burst out just when she was getting to the crucial bit in her group portrait. OK, so it meant she had to turn Stella into a giant monster with two heads, and Dahlia looked more like one of the pigs, but it was still SOOO funny! At least me and Luca thought so.

Anyway, this time all the gang are just going to love it. In fact, they'll totes TWEET OUT LOUD, even if I do say so myself.

Right. Wish me luck, dear Diary. Not that I'm going to need it. I mean, I'm Poppy, Pranking Queen of the Island, the Prankster Extraordinaire herself. What could POSSIBLY go wrong?

5PM

A lot, apparently. Like a HUMONGOUS lot. Like, imagine the most MAHOOSIVE thing you can possibly think of. And then quadruple it.

And that is still only HALF the amount of utter wrongness that just happened.

Oh, Diary, I can't even bring myself to tell you the details, but let's just say that a whole heap of things are a bit broken, Stella and Willow aren't speaking to each other, and Dahlia says I'm not allowed to even LOOK at her test tubes ever again in my entire life.

But, worst of all, I've been banned from pranking until next Sunday. That's, like, a whole week. Which is, like, FOREVER. I mean, how am I supposed to have any fun at all round here if I'm not thinking up even an itty-bitty little trick or two? Stella said they've put up with the pranks for long enough and it was about time I realised it's not ALL about me. I said I wasn't doing it for me, I was doing it for THEM. Only she pointed out that so far this month my pranks had left her with four missing spoons, a broken skateboard and a stain on the wall from where the pink flour bomb hit it that just WON'T wash off, so it wasn't really working out that well for her at all.

Plus Dahlia is tired of the endless racket, and how is she supposed to invent something as GENIUS as the wheel or sliced bread with a pain in the birdbrain? And Willow says that, even though she loves me more than the moon and stars themselves, I do 'have a tendency to ripple the biorhythms of the fragile island ecosystem with my desire for disturbance', which, like, I don't even UNDERSTAND. At least Luca thought it was funny! Though, to be fair, Luca thinks everything is funny.

I mean, I suppose Stella has a point. The pranks do sometimes, just SOMETIMES, have a habit of going a bit wrong. But, still, why couldn't Stella have just made me wash the dishes for a day, or fill in some pig holes, or have confiscated my drumsticks? Well, she confiscated those as well, but if she hadn't banned me from pranking I could probably have 'borrowed' something from Willow or Dahlia to use instead. I even said sorry a hundred-and-thirty-three times (Dahlia counted), but not even that was enough to change Stella's mind.

It's NOT FAIR. I mean, asking me not to prank is like asking Dahlia not to THINK or Stella not to SING or Willow not to do all the bazillion things Willow does. Or the pigs not to EAT or Gale not to LOOK IN THE MIRROR. Which, like, HELLO!

This is worse than the time I broke my cymbals and had to use two plastic plates instead, which do not have the same sound, no matter what Willow says.

AND the time I thought I'd lost Luca down the volcano after firing him from my slingshot and spent four hours looking for him.

(It turned out he'd flown straight over and was back in his treehouse playing pigs and ladders).

AND the time I ACCIDENTALLY exploded my own treehouse and had to share with Dahlia while she rebuilt it. Which wouldn't have been so bad except she TOTES talks in her sleep AND hogs the bed. I fell off twelve times and in the end I just slept inside the bass drum, which, to be fair, is where I've stayed ever since, but even so it was completely ANNOYING. Only not as annoying as today.

Today is, without doubt, the WORST DAY EVER. This is so HUMONGOUSLY AWFUL that I really think the WORLD IS ENDING. That, or it has to be a dream. Yes, that's it. There is no way that something this TOTES TRAGIC is actually happening to me. In fact, I'm going to go to bed right now and when I wake up tomorrow everything will be back to normal. And I, Poppy, the Queen of Pranksters, will be back to my usual tricks ...

MASTER THE SUPERPOWERS OF THE FEARLESS FLOCK, IN OVER 120 ACTION-PACKED LEVELS!

EGMONT
E2213